EXPLORING THE UNIVERSE

THE FAR PLANETS

ROBIN KERROD

RAINTREE
STECK-VAUGHN
RSVP® PUBLISHERS

A Harcourt Company

Austin   New York
www.raintreesteckvaughn.com

**First American edition published in 2002
by Raintree Steck-Vaughn Publishers**

© 2002 by Graham Beehag Books

Raintree Steck-Vaughn Publishers
4515 Seton Center Parkway
Austin, Texas 78755

Website address: www.raintreesteckvaughn.com

Library of Congress Cataloging-in-Publication Data

Data is available upon request

ISBN 0-7398-2820-7

Printed and bound in the United States.

1 2 3 4 5 6 7 8 9 0 05 04 03 02 01

Contents

EXPLORING THE FAR PLANETS

Saturn and its moons, a montage of images prepared from *Voyager 1*. Clockwise, the moons are as follows: Dione (in front of Saturn), Enceladus, Rhea, Titan, Mimas, and Tethys.

Introduction

Earth is one of nine bodies that are called planets, which circle, or orbit, the Sun. With thousands of other bodies, the planets make up what is known as the solar system. These other bodies include large lumps of rock and metal called asteroids and icy bodies called comets, which occasionally blaze across our skies.

In distance from the Sun, with the nearest listed first, the planets are Mercury, Venus, Earth, Mars, Jupiter, Saturn, Uranus, Neptune, and Pluto. Earth and its three closest neighbors among the planets—Mercury, Venus, and Mars—lie relatively close together in the heart of the solar system. These planets are separated from each other by several tens of millions of miles, which in space is considered a relatively short distance. Together, they are often referred to as the near or inner planets.

Hundreds of millions of miles separate them and Jupiter, the next planet out. The planets beyond Jupiter are even farther away. Together, Jupiter, Saturn, Uranus, Neptune, and Pluto are referred to as the far or outer planets.

The outer planets differ greatly from the inner planets. The inner planets are small, and most of the outer planets are giant. The inner planets are rocky, and most of the outer planets are made up of gas and liquid. The inner planets have only three moons between them, but the outer planets have more than 60. Most of the outer planets have rings around them, and the inner planets do not.

Although Jupiter is very far from Earth, it is so big that we can see it shining brightly in the sky for many months of the year. When its orbit brings it close to Earth, Saturn also shines brightly in the sky, in part because of its magnificent rings. Both planets were known to ancient stargazers. But the three most distant planets were not. They are too far away to be clearly visible to the naked eye. Uranus was not discovered until 1781, Neptune not until 1846, and Pluto not until 1930.

Paths of the Planets

The five outer planets—Jupiter, Saturn, Uranus, Neptune, and Pluto—occupy a vast region of space. They are far apart. Saturn never comes closer to Jupiter than about 400 million miles (640 million km). Neptune never comes closer to Uranus than about 1 billion miles (1.6 billion km).

The farther out the planets are, the longer is their "year"—the time it takes to complete one orbit around the Sun. Their "years" vary from just under 12 Earth-years for Jupiter to more than 248 Earth-years for Pluto.

Oval Orbits

All the planets orbit the Sun not in circles but in paths that are oval, or elliptical, in shape. The orbits of all the outer planets except Pluto are only slightly oval—they are nearly circular. But Pluto's orbit is very oval. This means that its distance from the Sun varies widely during the course of its year. Sometimes it gets within 2.8 billion miles (4.5 billion km) of the Sun. At other times it wanders more than 4.5 billion miles (7.4 billion km) away.

Pluto's orbit is unusual in another way. All the other outer planets circle the Sun in much the same plane (flat sheet) in space. But Pluto travels quite a long way above and below this plane.

Outer Planets

The five outer planets are widely scattered in space. Like the inner planets, they all orbit the Sun in the same direction.

Inner Planets

The four inner planets occupy only a tiny region at the center of the solar system. They are separated from the outer planets by the asteroid belt.

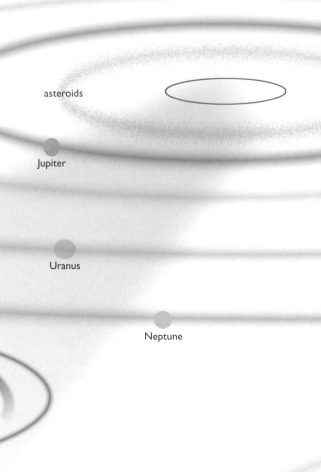

asteroids

Jupiter

Uranus

Neptune

Venus

Mercury

Sun

Earth

Mars

Planet Data

Planet	Av. distance from Sun million miles (km)	Diameter at equator in miles (km)	Completes Orbit (Length of Year)	Rotates around in (Length of Day)	Mass (Earth=1)	Density (water=1)	Number of moons
Jupiter	483 (778)	88,850 (142,980)	11.9 years	9.39 hours	318	1.3	16
Saturn	888 (1,429)	74,900 (120,540)	29.4 years	10.66 hours	95	0.7	18
Uranus	1,787 (2,875)	31,765 (51,120)	83.7 years	17.24 hours	15	1.3	18
Neptune	2,799 (4,504)	30,779 (49,530)	163.7 years	16.11 hours	17	1.6	8
Sun	—	865,000 (1,392,000)	—	25 days	330,000	1.4	—
Earth	93 (150)	7,927 (12,756)	1 year	23.93 hours	1	5.5	1

Pluto

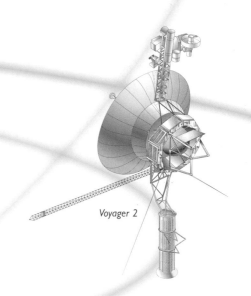

Voyager 2

Saturn

Exploring the Outer Planets

Considering how far away the outer planets are, we know an amazing amount about them. For example, we know that Jupiter's moon Io has active volcanoes. Saturn's rings are made up of millions of ringlets. Neptune has white-flecked clouds scurrying through its deep blue atmosphere. We have learned these things—and many others— from unmanned space probes that have explored the planets close-up.

Pioneer 10 was the first probe to travel to Jupiter. *Pioneer 11* visited Saturn as well. But most of our knowledge of the outer planets has come from the *Voyager 1* and *2* probes. Both were launched in 1977 and both visited Jupiter (1979) and Saturn (*Voyager 1* in 1980, *Voyager 2* in 1981). Then *Voyager 2* went on to fly by Uranus (1986) and Neptune (1989). No probes have yet reached Pluto.

Size and Structure

The outer planets are very different in size and make-up from the inner planets. Four of them—Jupiter, Saturn, Uranus, and Neptune—are often called gas giants because of their huge size and because they are made up mainly of gas. They have no solid surface. Pluto is different—it is a tiny ball of rock and ice.

Jupiter and Saturn are by far the biggest planets, and they have a similar make-up. They have a relatively thin layer of atmosphere, made up mainly of the gases hydrogen and helium. At the bottom of the atmosphere, high pressure forces the hydrogen gas to a liquid. Deeper down, even higher pressure turns the liquid hydrogen into a kind of liquid metal. This liquid metallic hydrogen reaches right down to the center, or core, of the planets, which is probably made up of dense rock.

The other gas giants, Uranus and Neptune, are similar both in size and in make-up. They have a deep atmosphere made up of hydrogen, helium, and methane gases. Underneath, there is a vast ocean made up of hot liquid containing water, methane, and ammonia. At the center, they have a small rocky core.

How the Gas Giants Formed

The solar system came into being about 4.6 billion years ago. That was when the Sun was born and the planets formed around it—both the small rocky inner ones and the giant, gassy outer ones. So how is it that the inner and outer planets came to be so different in structure? Astronomers think that this happened soon after the Sun became a star.

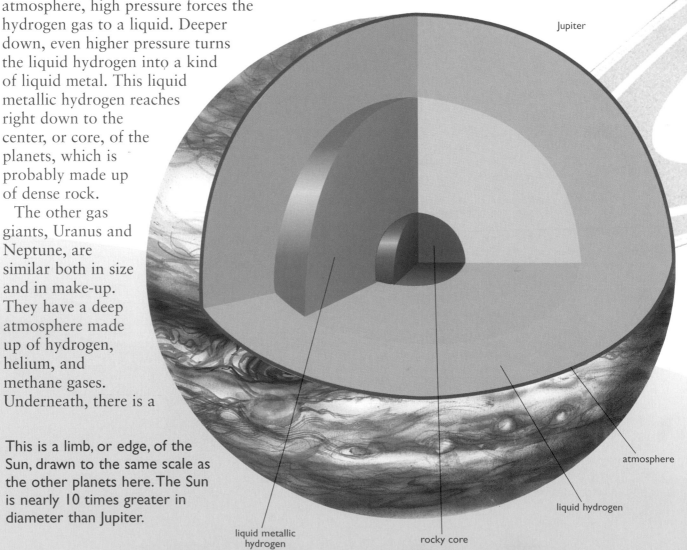

Jupiter

This is a limb, or edge, of the Sun, drawn to the same scale as the other planets here. The Sun is nearly 10 times greater in diameter than Jupiter.

Sun

atmosphere

liquid hydrogen

liquid metallic hydrogen

rocky core

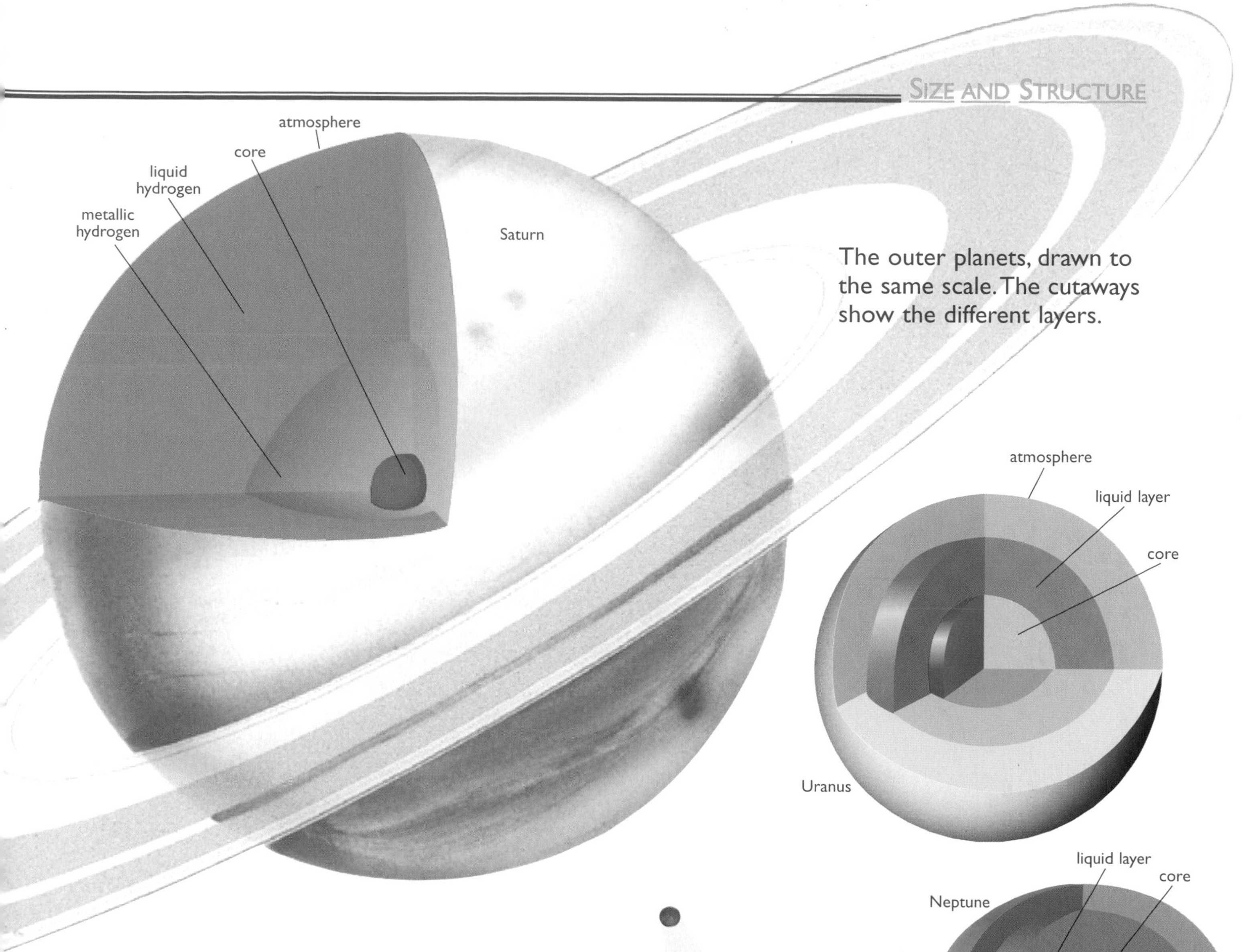

atmosphere

liquid
hydrogen

core

metallic
hydrogen

Saturn

The outer planets, drawn to
the same scale. The cutaways
show the different layers.

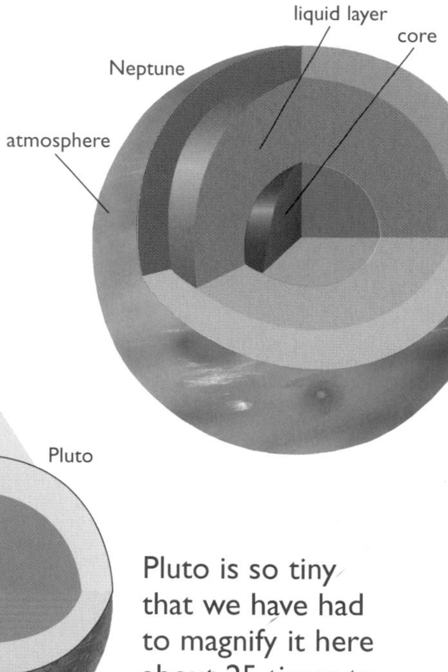

atmosphere

liquid layer

core

Uranus

liquid layer

core

Neptune

atmosphere

frozen methane,
nitrogen, and carbon
monoxide

frozen
water ice

Pluto

core

In the process, the Sun blasted off its outer
layers. The blast of matter blew like a
mighty wind through the young solar
system. It stripped away the gassy
atmospheres from around the nearby inner
planets, leaving them bare. The outer
planets were not so affected in the same way
because they were much farther away from
the Sun. They kept their original
atmospheres, and their gravity, or pull, and
gradually attracted more and more of the
gas that had been blasted out of the inner
solar system. Over time, they grew into the
giant bodies we find today.

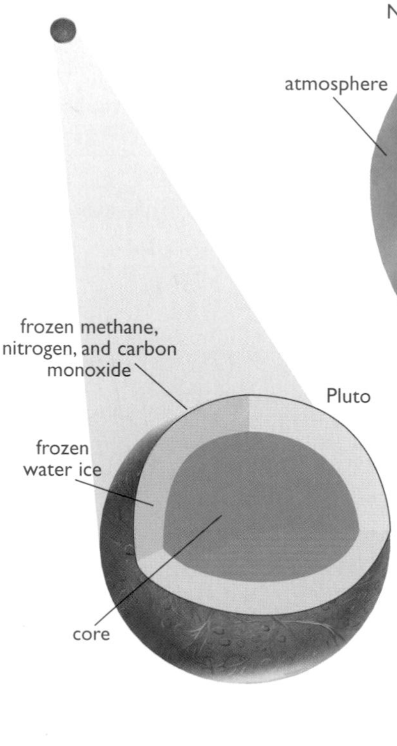

Pluto is so tiny
that we have had
to magnify it here
about 25 times to
show its makeup.

GIANT JUPITER

Jupiter is by far the largest of the planets. A gigantic ball of gas and liquid, Jupiter is more than 11 times greater in diameter than Earth. It could fit within itself 1,300 bodies the size of Earth. Jupiter is named after the king of the gods in Roman mythology, and in terms of size it is the "king" of the planets.

Jupiter is the fifth planet in the solar system in distance from the Sun. It circles around the Sun at an average distance of about 500 million miles (800 million km) and takes nearly 12 years to circle the Sun once. Jupiter lies between the nearer planet Mars and the more distant Saturn, but the closest bodies to it are the smaller bodies known as asteroids. They circle the Sun in a broad ring, or belt, roughly halfway between the orbits of Mars and Jupiter.

Even though Jupiter never comes closer to Earth than about 400 million miles (640 million km), it shines brightly in the night sky. To people on Earth it appears as a brilliant white "star" during many months of the year. The brightest object in the night sky after the Moon and Venus, it far outshines the "real" stars. Mars can sometimes rival Jupiter in brightness, but it can easily be distinguished from Jupiter by its fiery orange or reddish color.

Jupiter is a good object for observation. Using ordinary binoculars, you can see it as a circle, or disk, and you may be able to spot four of its moons as points of light on either side. This reminds us that Jupiter is the center of its own miniature system of heavenly bodies, with at least 16 moons circling around it.

Through a telescope, Jupiter looks magnificent. Its disk is crossed with colored bands and dotted with spots. When you watch the planet for some time, you can see the spots and other features move across the disk. This shows that Jupiter is spinning around very rapidly. Observations show that it spins, or rotates, completely on its axis in less than 10 hours—faster than any other planet. The period of time that it takes Jupiter (or any other planet) to complete a single rotation is the length of its day.

Left: Jupiter's moon Io is more brilliantly colored than any other moon in the solar system.

White and reddish-orange bands of clouds fill Jupiter's thick atmosphere. Between these bands are great turbulent regions where currents in the atmosphere eddy this way and that. It is in these regions that violent storms take place.

The Belts and Zones

Space probes such as *Pioneer 10* and *11*, the two Voyagers, and Galileo have studied Jupiter in detail. They have shown that the colored bands on Jupiter's disk are fast-moving clouds high in the planet's atmosphere.

The clouds have been drawn into parallel bands because the atmosphere moves so quickly. Astronomers call the dark bands of clouds "belts" and the light ones "zones."

The Cloud Layers

The main gases in Jupiter's atmosphere are hydrogen and helium. There is also a little methane. The pale cloud bands seem to be made up of icy crystals of ammonia. The dark cloud bands seem to be made up of compounds of ammonia and sulfur. They are lower than the ammonia clouds.

Above: The colorful face of Jupiter is crossed by dark belts and light zones. Dark and light spots show where there are stormy regions.

Left: Cloud layers in Jupiter's atmosphere.

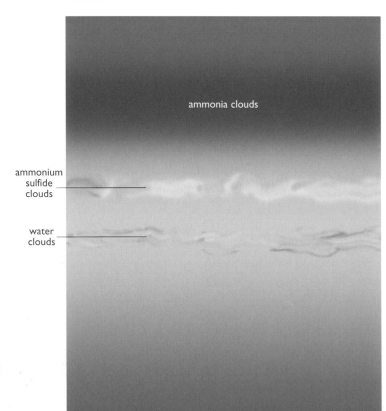

ammonia clouds

ammonium sulfide clouds

water clouds

Between the the main cloud layers there seems to be a haze of water-ice crystals. They are similar to the icy cirrus clouds on Earth, which are sometimes called mares' tails.

Furious Winds

The winds within the belts and zones travel at different speeds. They blow fastest around the equator and slow down to the north and south. Around the equator they can reach speeds of up to about 350 miles (560 km) an hour, more than the wind speed in a tornado on Earth.

The winds in the belts and zones also travel in different directions. Some blow toward the east, others toward the west.

JUPITER DATA

Diameter: 88,850 miles (142,980 km)

Average distance from Sun: 483,000,000 miles (778,000,000 km)

Mass (Earth=1): 318

Density (water=1): 1.3

Spins on axis in: 9.93 days

Circles around Sun in: 11.9 years

Number of moons: 16

across as Earth and is known as the Great Red Spot. Astronomers have observed it for more than 300 years. It seems to be a region of high pressure in which spiraling winds carry gases high above the usual cloud layers. Its color seems to come from compounds of phosphorus, a chemical element found on Earth that is often used in manufacturing matches.

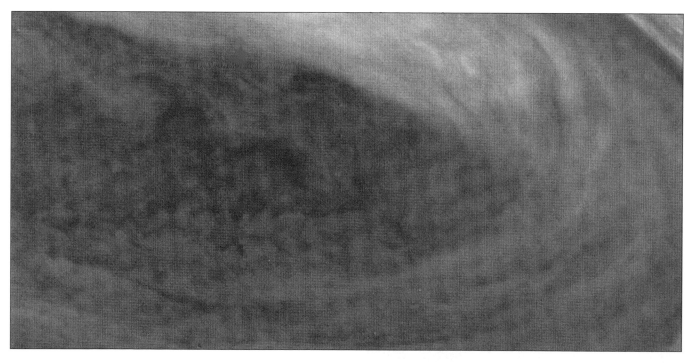

Stormy Weather

Where the winds moving west meet the winds moving east, the result is an even greater disturbance, or turbulence, in the atmosphere. As a result of this turbulence, great waves form in Jupiter's atmosphere. Furious hurricane-like storms break out. They appear to observers on Earth as pale and dark ovals.

The biggest one is a huge red oval region found in one of the cloud bands in Jupiter's southern hemisphere. It is three times as big

Above: Furious winds swirl around in Jupiter's Great Red Spot, which measures more than 25,000 miles (40,000 km) across.

Below: Makeup of Jupiter's cloudy atmosphere. It is mainly hydrogen and helium.

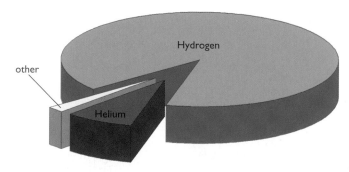

As we saw earlier (page 8), Jupiter is made up mainly of hydrogen in three different forms. The atmosphere contains hydrogen gas. Beneath this there are deep layers of hydrogen in the form of a liquid and then in the form of a liquid metal.

All of Jupiter spins around very rapidly—its atmosphere, its liquid hydrogen ocean, and its liquid metal layer. But when metal moves, electric currents are created. These electric currents generate the force we call magnetism.

So, as the liquid metal in Jupiter moves with the planet's rotation, electric currents are created inside it, and giving the planet its magnetic field. Earth gets its magnetism in a similar way, because of electric currents set up in its metal core.

Jupiter's magnetism is much more powerful than Earth's and reaches out

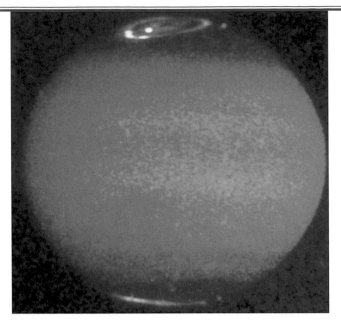

Above: Particles from Jupiter's radiation belts spill into its atmosphere and create auroras—glowing light displays around the north and south poles.

Below: Jupiter's magnetism shields the planet from the solar wind.

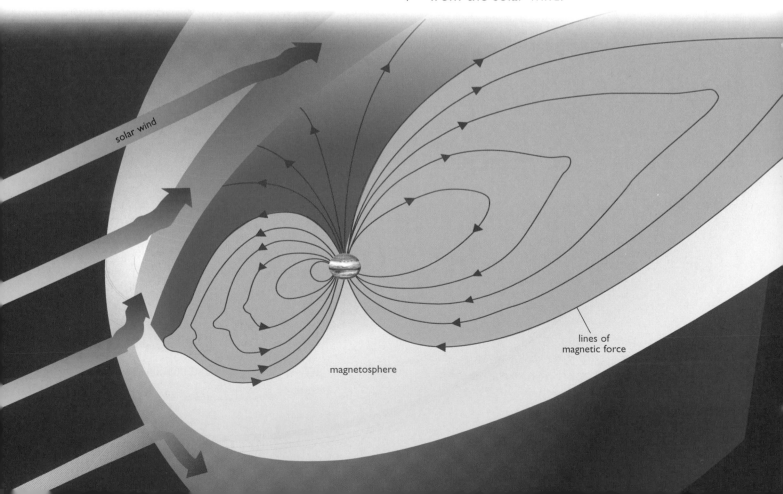

solar wind

magnetosphere

lines of magnetic force

millions of miles into space. It traps tiny electrical particles that pour into space from the Sun to form regions, or belts, of radiation. Earth has similar regions, called the Van Allen belts. The radiation from Jupiter's belts pose a great danger to spacecraft and could be deadly to any human crew.

Rings Around Jupiter

The Voyager space probes discovered many new things about Jupiter when they flew past the planet in 1979. One of their most unexpected discoveries was that Jupiter has a set of rings circling its equator it. They are much fainter than Saturn's famous rings and cannot be seen from Earth.

Jupiter's main ring is located about 40,000 miles (64,000 km) from the planet's cloud tops. This ring circles Jupiter around the orbits of the two nearest of the planet's moons—tiny Adrastea and Metis.

The main ring measures about 4,300 miles (7,000 km) across, but it is less than 20 miles (32 km) thick. It is made up of very tiny grains of dust, something like the smoke from bonfires on Earth.

Other rings are found both inside and outside the main ring. The inner ring is much fainter, but thicker, and is known as the halo. The outer ring is even fainter and is called the gossamer ring. Two more moons—Amalthea and Thebe—orbit inside the ring. Astronomers believe that the ring is made up of particles chipped off the two moons.

Jupiter's rings (right) are too faint to be seen from Earth. The very faint gossamer ring extends far beyond the main one, even beyond the orbits of the moons Amalthea and Thebe.

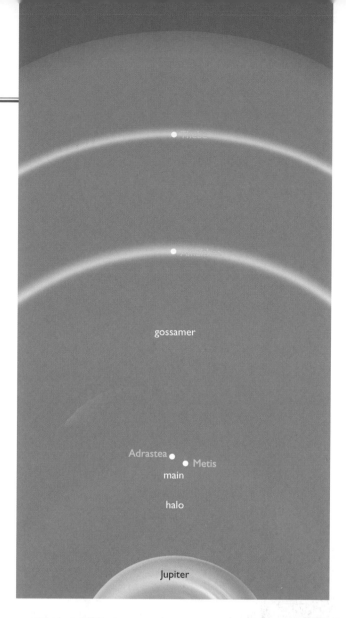

gossamer

Adrastea● ●Metis
main

halo

Jupiter

Many Moons

In January 1610, the Italian astronomer Galileo trained his newly built telescope on Jupiter. He saw little points of light like stars lined up on either side of the planet. These "stars" changed their position from night to night. He realized that they were tiny satellites, or moons, of Jupiter, circling in orbit around it. There were four moons in all.

These four moons can be seen through binoculars or a small telescope. We call them the Galilean moons in honor of their discoverer. In order of distance from Jupiter, they are Io, Europa, Ganymede, and Callisto. Over the centuries, using telescopes astronomers discovered another nine smaller moons farther away from the planet. The Voyager space probes found three more, making a total of 16 moons in all.

Satellite Groups

The 16 moons of Jupiter divide neatly into three groups, widely separated from each other. The four Galilean moons form part of the inner group of eight moons. The other four in this group are much smaller than Io and lie closer to Jupiter. Callisto, the outermost of the inner group, orbits about 1,200,000 miles (1,900,000 km) from Jupiter.

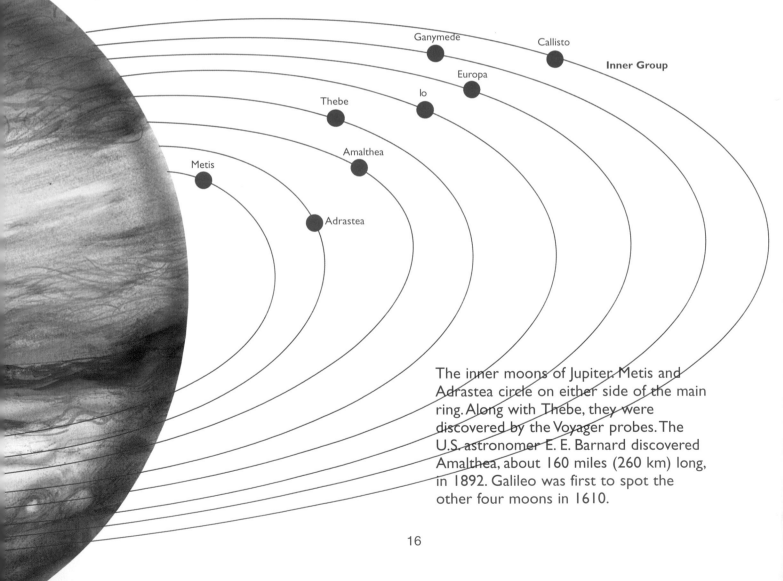

The inner moons of Jupiter Metis and Adrastea circle on either side of the main ring. Along with Thebe, they were discovered by the Voyager probes. The U.S. astronomer E. E. Barnard discovered Amalthea, about 160 miles (260 km) long, in 1892. Galileo was first to spot the other four moons in 1610.

Moon

Europa

Io

Callisto

Ganymede

Earth

Above: Jupiter's four Galilean moons, compared in size with the Earth and our own Moon.

Four moons make up a middle group, which is about seven times farther away from the planet. The innermost of these moons, called Leda, measures only about 6 miles (10 km) across. It is the smallest of all Jupiter's moons.

The outer group of four moons is twice as far away as the middle group. They orbit around Jupiter in the opposite direction of the others. Scientists say they have retrograde motion. The outermost of these moons, called Sinope, wanders as far as 15,000,000 miles (24,000,000 km) from Jupiter. It takes over two years to travel around the planet.

The Trojans

Jupiter's powerful gravity holds its family of moons. The planet's gravitational field also captured two groups of asteroids from the nearby asteroid belt. Both groups circle the Sun in the same orbit as Jupiter, one in front of the planet and one behind.

These asteroid groups are called the Trojans. Each has been named after figures from the Trojan War, which the ancient Greeks fought against Troy, a city-state in what is now Turkey. The two largest are Hector, which is about 120 miles (190 km) in width, and Agamemnon, which is slightly smaller.

Leda

Middle Group

Himalia

Lysithea

Elara

The middle group of Jupiter's moons, which all orbit more than 7 million miles (11 million km) from the planet. Tiny Leda was not discovered by telescope until 1974. Of this group, Himalia (105 miles, 170 km across) is the biggest.

The Galilean Moons

The four Galilean moons dwarf Jupiter's other 12 moons and most other moons in the solar system. With a diameter of 3,273 miles (5,268 km), Ganymede is bigger even than the planet Mercury. Callisto is about the same size as Mercury, while Io is a little larger and Europa a little smaller than our own Moon.

Although they are relatively close together in space and are similar in size, the Galilean moons differ in composition and appearance.

Makeup of the Moons

Scientists think that Io has a solid core that is rich in iron. Io's core is surrounded by a thick layer of molten rock. On top is a thin, hard, rocky outer layer, or crust.

Europa also has an iron-rich core, surrounded by a thick layer of solid rock. Above this there is probably a deep ocean of water, with a layer of ice on top.

Ganymede also has an icy crust, with thick layers of ice and rock underneath. In the center, there is an iron core, which may be partly molten.

Most of Callisto consists of a solid mixture of rock and ice, with no distinct layers. Its surface is icy, too.

The Ice Moons

Europa, Ganymede, and Callisto all have an icy surface but look quite different. Europa is amazingly smooth and bright—indeed, it is one of the brightest bodies in the solar system. Ganymede is covered in dark and pale regions, while Callisto is dark all over.

Below: The probable makeup of the four Galilean moons. They are all different. Much of Io is made up of molten rock. Europa may have an ocean of water under its surface.

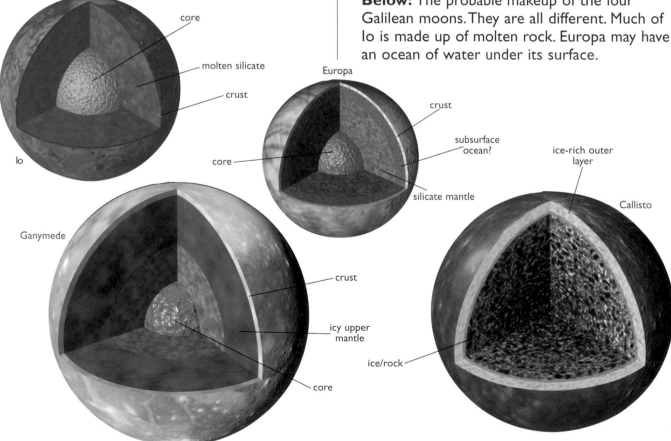

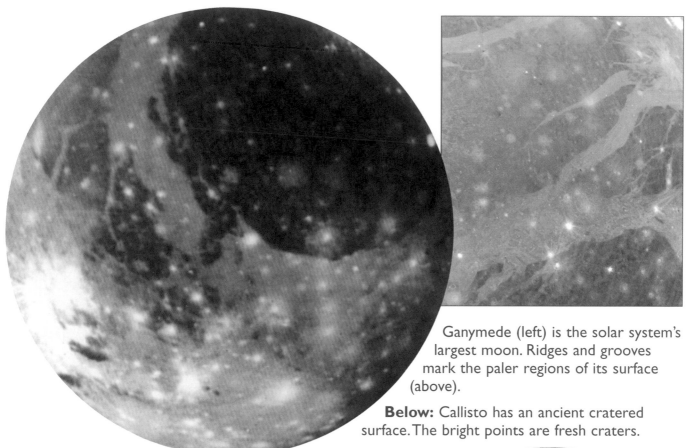

Ganymede (left) is the solar system's largest moon. Ridges and grooves mark the paler regions of its surface (above).

Below: Callisto has an ancient cratered surface. The bright points are fresh craters.

Callisto's somber surface is pitted with craters, dug when meteorites or asteroids bombarded it long ago. The presence of so many craters on the surface indicates that Io must be very old. Here and there, white patches show where recent meteorite hits have thrown out fresh ice from craters.

Ganymede's surface is also marked with craters. There are more craters in the dark regions, which indicates that they are older than the brighter regions. The brighter regions are lighter in color because they contain fresher ice than the darker regions. They are crisscrossed by sets of parallel ridges and valleys that are up to tens of miles wide and hundreds of miles long. This kind of feature is known as grooved terrain. It probably formed when the surface stretched and cracked.

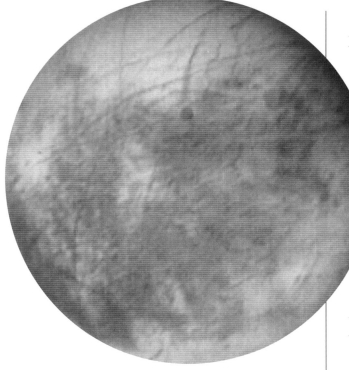

Europa has a smoother surface than any other moon.

Fascinating Europa

The Voyager space probes gave us our first views of the smallest Galilean moon, Europa. Images from the Voyager probe indicated that Europa has a very smooth icy surface, crisscrossed by a network of darker lines. The superior images sent back by a more recent probe, *Galileo*, have revealed a much more complex surface.

Galileo has shown that Europa has bright plains and darker mottled terrain, cut by networks of narrow ridges and grooves. These seem to be fractures, or breaks, in the icy surface. Scattered here and there are blocks of ice that appear to have broken free and drifted to new positions, like ice floes do in the Arctic Ocean on Earth.

Few craters are visible on Europa, suggesting that it has a very young surface. The craters that are present are not as prominent as those on the other moons. As meteorites hit the surface, the craters they make quickly fill with slushy material. They often appear darker than their surroundings because of material that wells up from under the icy surface.

In other parts of Europa domes and smooth areas known as puddles are found. These features could be caused by hot spots beneath the surface. Ultimately such sources could melt the ice beneath the surface and create an ocean of liquid water. Scientists have suggested that if there is an ocean of water, then Io's surface might contain some primitive forms of life.

Below: Fascinating patterns show up in the ice that forms the surface of Europa.

gas itself but of sulfur dioxide snow—sulfur dioxide that turns into icy crystals in the cold vacuum of space.

More than 80 active volcanoes have been spotted on Io, and there are many craters where volcanoes have erupted in the past. All Io's volcanoes are named after mythological fire gods and goddesses or other fiery subjects. The first volcano spotted on Io, Pele, was named for the legendary Hawaiian volcano goddess.

Left: In this Voyager picture, Io (left) and Europa are seen with Jupiter in the background.

Amazing Io

Io has the most unusual surface of all the Galilean moons. Io's surface is not dull and drab or ice-covered but vividly colored in shades of yellow, orange, black, and white. We see little of the hard outer rocky crust of Io because it is covered almost entirely in the chemical element sulfur. Sulfur can be found in a variety of yellow and orange forms.

Where does this sulfur come from? On Io, it comes from erupting volcanoes. These volcanoes pour out molten sulfur and some molten rock as well. On Earth, volcanoes pour out mainly molten rock.

Earth volcanoes also give off gases, including sulfur dioxide. On Io, the volcanoes give off huge volumes of sulfur dioxide. In Io's low gravity, the gas shoots high above the surface, creating beautiful fountain-like streams, or plumes. The plumes we see in photographs are not of the

Volcanoes are always erupting on Io, one of the most geologically active bodies in the solar system.

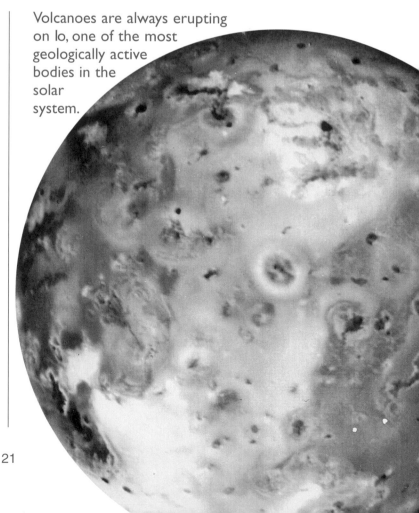

STUNNING SATURN

Through a telescope, Saturn appears perhaps the most beautiful planet of all because of the brilliant rings that circle it. It is the second-largest planet in the solar system, about four-fifths the size of Jupiter and nearly 10 times greater in diameter than Earth.

Saturn circles the Sun at an average distance of about 890 million miles (1,430 million km). It is the most distant planet that can be easily seen in the night sky with the naked eye.

From Earth, Saturn appears as a yellowish star. It never shines as bright in the night sky as Jupiter because it is much farther away—it never gets closer to Earth than about 800 million miles (1,300 million km). Its brightness in the sky varies greatly. Sometimes it shines more brilliantly than all the stars in the sky except Sirius and Canopus. But at other times it looks quite dim and is difficult to find among the true stars.

In make-up, Saturn is much like Jupiter, with an atmosphere of hydrogen and helium. Underneath, there are layers of hydrogen in the form of a liquid and in the form of a liquid metal. However, Saturn is much lighter for its size than Jupiter—it has a much lower density. Indeed, its density is lower than that of water. So if you could drop Saturn into a large enough bowl of water, it would float. No other planet would do this.

The face, or disk, of Saturn we see in a telescope is not as colorful as Jupiter's. We see similar bands of clouds traveling parallel to the planet's equator, but they are much fainter. The most noticeable feature of the disk is the dark shadow cast by the rings, which circle Saturn's equator.

All four giant outer planets have rings, but only Saturn's can easily be seen from Earth. Saturn's rings appear brighter than other planets' rings because they are broader and denser and because they are made up of icy particles not dark dusty matter.

Left: The surface of Enceladus, one of Saturn's many moons. Like Jupiter's large moons, it seems to have an icy surface, pitted with craters.

22

Saturn with two of its moons visible.
The face of the planet shows bands of
clouds, but it is much hazier than
Jupiter's face. The three classic rings
show up clearly here—C, B, and A
moving outward from the planet.

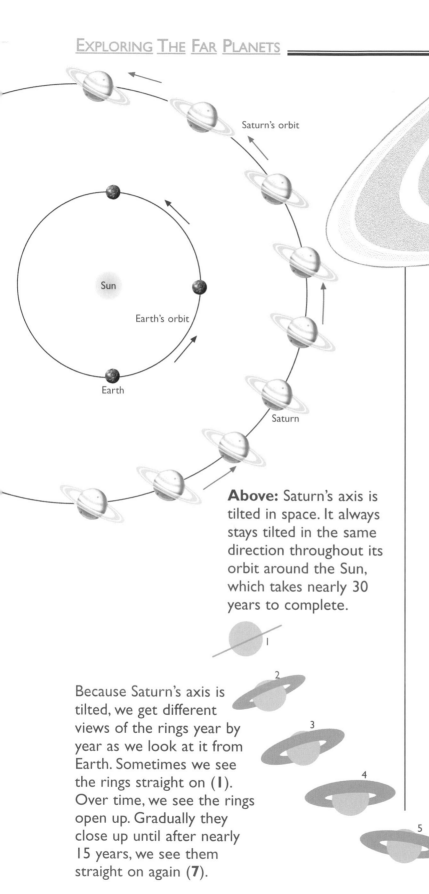

Saturn's orbit

Sun

Earth's orbit

Earth

Saturn

Above: Saturn's axis is tilted in space. It always stays tilted in the same direction throughout its orbit around the Sun, which takes nearly 30 years to complete.

Because Saturn's axis is tilted, we get different views of the rings year by year as we look at it from Earth. Sometimes we see the rings straight on (**1**). Over time, we see the rings open up. Gradually they close up until after nearly 15 years, we see them straight on again (**7**).

SATURN DATA

Diameter: 74,900 miles (120,540 km)
Average distance from Sun: 888,000,000 miles (1,429,000,000 km)
Mass (Earth=1): 95
Density (water=1): 0.7
Spins on axis in: 10.66 days
Circles around Sun in: 29.4 years
Number of moons: 18

Spinning Around

Like all the planets, Saturn moves in two ways. It both travels in space in an elliptical orbit around the Sun and it spins around, or rotates, on its axis. The length of time that it takes to complete a single rotation is the length of Saturn's day.

Saturn spins around in space very rapidly, rotating once in about 10½ hours. Among the planets, only Jupiter spins around faster. This rapid spinning causes Saturn to bulge out noticeably at the equator and flatten out at the poles. The planet becomes misshapen in this way because it is made up of fluid (gas and liquid), and fluids can change their shape easily.

Magnetic Saturn

Like Jupiter, Saturn contains a thick layer of liquid hydrogen in the form of a metal. As this metal layer spins around with the planet, it creates electrical currents and magnetism (see page 14). Saturn does not have as strong a metallic pull as Jupiter.

Saturn's Year

Saturn takes nearly 30 Earth-years to circle once around the Sun. During this time we get different views of the planet because of the way it spins around in space. It does not spin in an upright position as it circles the Sun. It spins around at an angle—its axis in space is tilted. (Earth's axis is tilted in space in a similar way.)

Because of the tilt of its axis, we view Saturn at a slightly different angle every year. In particular, we see slightly different views of its rings. When the planet's axis is tilted most toward us, we get the clearest view of the rings' circular openings. Saturn's axis is tilted in a different direction, we see the rings from the side, which makes them almost invisible.

Atmosphere and Weather

Saturn has a hazy, cloudy atmosphere. The clouds speed around the planet in parallel bands. The darker bands are called "belts," and the lighter ones, "zones." Within the bands, the winds blow mainly toward the east, following the planet's direction of rotation. In some bands the winds blow in the opposite direction, toward the west.

The strongest winds blow around the equator, where they can reach speeds of

The Hubble Space Telescope spotted this violent storm raging in Saturn's atmosphere.

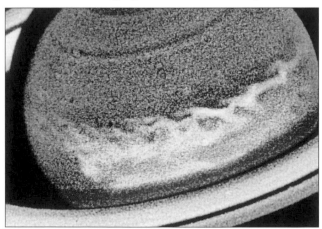

more than 1,100 mph (1,800 km/h). This is about five times the speed of the strongest hurricane winds on Earth.

Where winds blowing toward the east meet winds blowing toward the west, the atmosphere experiences turbulence. Great hurricane-like storms are formed. From Earth they appear as pale, dark patches or spots. Some of these features last for years. One discovered by the Voyager probes, named Anne's Spot, was deep red, like Jupiter's Great Red Spot but much smaller.

Makeup of Saturn's atmosphere. Like Jupiter's, it is mainly hydrogen and helium.

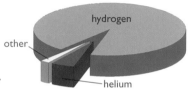

Below: Cloud layers in Saturn's atmosphere.

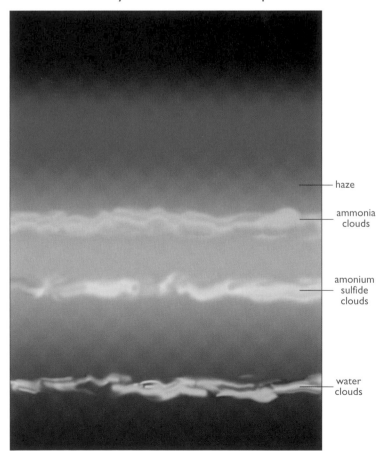

haze

ammonia clouds

amonium sulfide clouds

water clouds

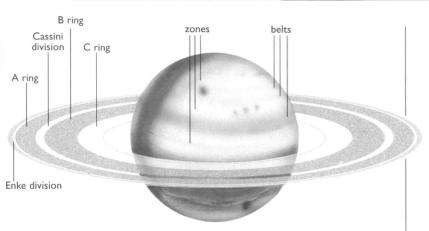

B ring
Cassini division
C ring
zones
belts
A ring
Enke division

Above: Features of Saturn and its rings that we can see from Earth—the bands of clouds, the three classic rings, and the two divisions.

The Glorious Rings

When the Italian astronomer Galileo first observed Saturn through a telescope in 1610, he noticed that there was something strange about the planet. The main body seemed to have "companions" on either side. What Galileo was seeing was the rings extending on each side of the planet, but his telescope was not powerful enough to show them as rings.

Later astronomers saw the rings more clearly but thought that they were solid. In 1875 the English scientist James Clerk Maxwell proved that solid rings could not exist because they would be torn apart by the forces set up by Saturn's enormous gravity. The rings had to be made up of separate lumps of material.

Simple as ABC
Through telescopes, Saturn appears to have three rings, named A (the outer), B, and C (the inner). The B ring is the brightest of the rings. It contains more matter than the other

Right: Closer-up, several more rings become visible. The very faint outer E ring surrounds the orbits of several of Saturn's large moons.

rings, which makes it reflect sunlight better. After the B ring, the A ring is brightest. The C ring is much fainter and contains so little matter that it is transparent.

From one side to the other, the visible ring system measures about 170,000 miles (274,000 km) across. The B ring is the widest of the rings, measuring some 15,000 miles (25,000 km) across. It is separated from the A ring by a dark gap, which is

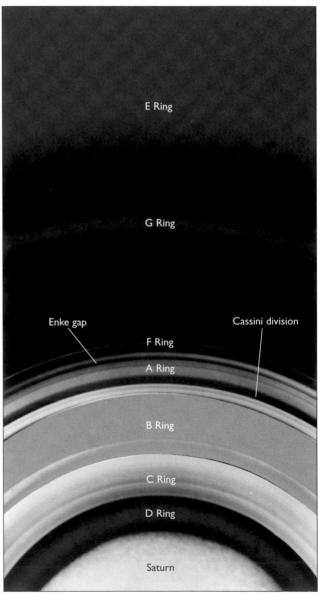

E Ring
G Ring
Enke gap
Cassini division
F Ring
A Ring
B Ring
C Ring
D Ring
Saturn

called the Cassini Division. There is also a narrower gap near the outer edge of the A ring, called the Encke Division.

New Rings and Ringlets

When the *Pioneer 11* and the two Voyager probes visited Saturn, they discovered several more rings. They found an even fainter ring inside the C ring. This D ring probably extends right down to Saturn's cloud tops.

The other rings lie outside the visible ring system. Close to the A ring lies a very narrow F ring. Farther out lie a broader but fainter G ring and beyond that a very broad and very faint E ring. The probes also showed that the three rings we see from Earth are made up of thousands upon thousands of separate ringlets.

One of the most beautiful images of Saturn and its rings sent back by the Voyager probes. The B ring shines brightest here. Like the other rings, it is made up of thousands of narrow ringlets.

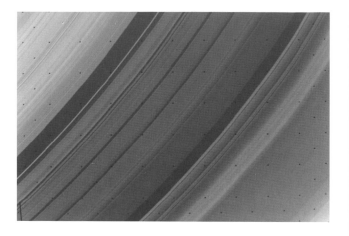

Above: The individual ringlets are produced by icy particles circling round the planet very quickly. Particles in the B ring, for example, circle Saturn in a little under 12 hours.

Below: By computer processing Voyager images into false-color pictures, the differences in particle sizes in the rings can be seen.

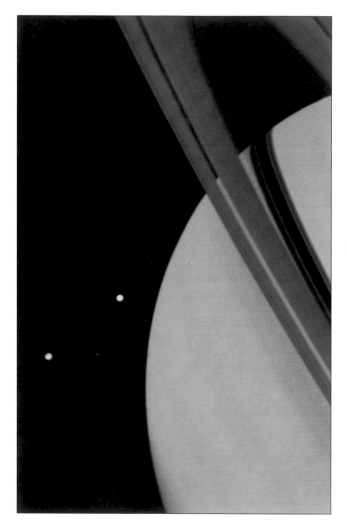

Above: Voyager spotted two of Saturn's moons close to the planet's limb. They are Tethys (top) and Dione, which are roughly the same size—about 700 miles (1,100 km) across.

Racing Around

The thousands of ringlets that together form Saturn's rings are made up of bits of matter that travel around the planet at high speed. These bits seem to be made up mainly of water ice, which is why the rings reflect light so well. The bits vary widely in size— some are smaller than pebbles, while others are as big as boulders, up to 33 feet (10 meters) across.

The Shepherds

Several of Saturn's many moons are found within the system of rings. The relatively large satellites Mimas and Enceladus, for example, circle the planet within the outer E ring. Of even greater interest are three tiny moons found on either side of the narrow F ring.

The smallest one circles close to the outer edge of the A ring. Named Atlas, it is no more than about 11 miles (18 km) in diameter. Astronomers believe that this tiny moon somehow helps keep the particles in the A ring in place. They call it a shepherd moon because it seems to "herd" the ring particles just as a shepherd herds a flock of sheep.

In a similar way, two small moons seem to keep the particles in the narrow F ring in place. These shepherd moons, named Pandora and Prometheus, orbit on either side of the ring.

Many More Moons

The three "shepherds" mentioned were among several new moons discovered by the Voyager probes. The probe found other small moons circling in the same orbits as some of the large moons that we can see from Earth, such as Tethys and Dione. Altogether Saturn has at least 18 known moons, and others have been glimpsed from time to time but not confirmed by repeated sightings.

Tethys and Dione form part of a group of inner moons around Saturn, which also includes Mimas and Enceladus, closer in, and Rhea, farther out. More than twice as far away from Saturn as Rhea are a pair of moons, vastly different in size. First comes Titan, more than 3,000 miles (5,000 km) in diameter, then Hyperion, which is only one-tenth Titan's size.

Far Apart

Saturn's two outer satellites are even more widely separated. Iapetus lies twice as far away from Saturn as Hyperion, while Phoebe lies nearly four times farther away.

Phoebe does not circle around Saturn in the same direction as the other moons. It circles in a clockwise direction. Astronomers say it has a retrograde orbit.

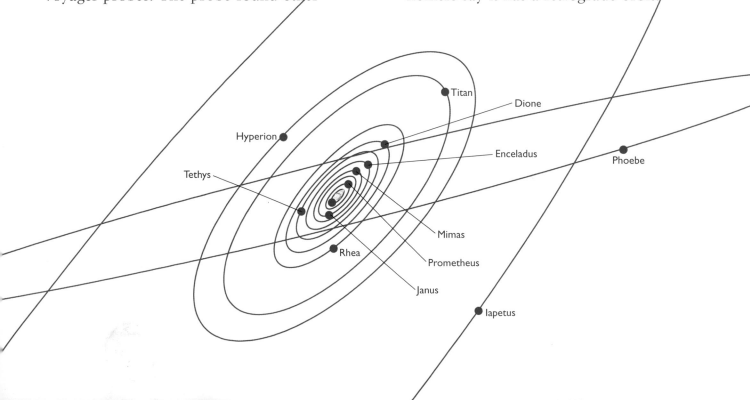

Mimas

Left: The cratered surface of Dione. The two largest craters here are Aeneas (bottom) and Dido (top). They both show the central peaks of the large craters on the Moon.

Dione

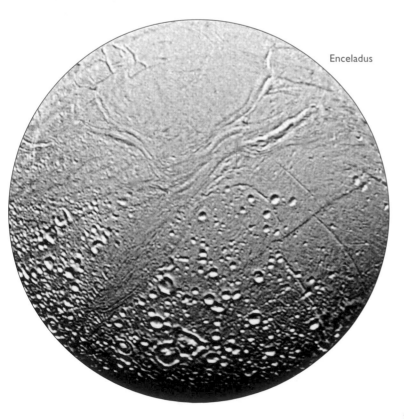

Enceladus

Icy Moons

The tiny moons of Saturn that space probes discovered are irregularly shaped lumps no bigger than about 130 miles (220 km) in diameter. They are probably made up of rock.

Most of Saturn's moons that can be seen from Earth are spherical, or ball-shaped. Most seem to be made up of a mixture of ice and rock, rather like the large moons of Jupiter. Most have an icy surface. The exception is Titan, which is very different from the others.

Saturn's icy moons might all be similar in make-up, but they all look different from one another. Mimas is the nearest large moon to Saturn. It is heavily cratered. Its largest crater, 80 miles (130 km) across, is named Herschel in honor of the English astronomer William Herschel, who discovered the moon in 1789.

Farther out and a little larger than Mimas is Enceladus. Its surface contains many large smooth regions. In places they are crossed by what look like ridges and valleys. These features were probably formed when the icy crust moved and cracked. It has fewer craters than Mimas, and they appear as though they formed quite recently. This suggests than Enceladus has quite a young surface that may still be changing.

Left: Enceladus has large, smooth plains as well as more heavily cratered regions. It looks particularly bright because it reflects almost all the sunlight that falls on it.

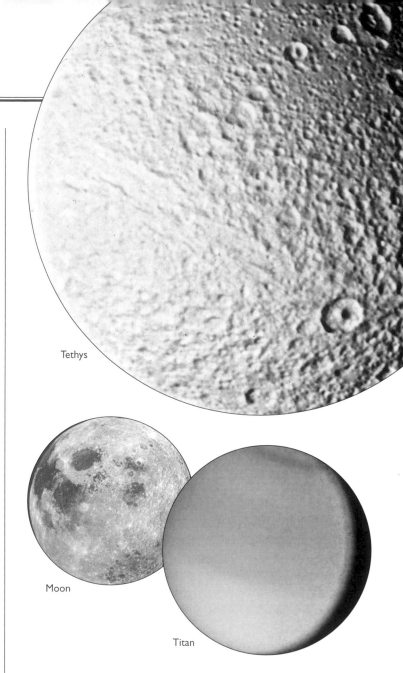

Left: Mimas was the first of Saturn's moons to be found, by William Herschel in 1789, eight years after he had discovered the planet Uranus. It measures about 250 miles (400 km) across.

Right: Tethys is heavily cratered and also has a long, deep valley cutting across it. You can see it in the picture, ending just before the prominent crater (Telemachus) near the bottom. The valley, named Ithaca Chasma, is about 1,200 miles (2,000 km) long.

Tethys

Moon

Titan

The next two icy moons beyond Enceladus are Tethys and Dione, which are roughly the same size. Next comes Rhea, which is 50 percent larger. All three moons are peppered with craters, although they also have smoother plains regions as well.

The most notable feature on Tethys is a huge valley system, known as Ithaca Chasma. Some 1,200 miles (2,000 km) long, it stretches three-quarters of the way around the moon.

Titan

Titan is by far Saturn's largest moon, with a diameter of 3,200 miles (5,150 km). This makes it larger than any other moon in the solar system except for Jupiter's Ganymede. It is bigger than the planet Mercury.

Astronomers think that Titan is made up of a mixture of rock and ice, like Saturn's other large moons. But it is much denser than the other moons, which means it contains more rocky matter.

We don't know what the surface of Titan looks like because the moon has a thick atmosphere. It is the only moon in the solar system to have one. The main gas in the atmosphere is nitrogen, which is also the main gas in Earth's atmosphere. Other gases in the atmosphere include methane (the gas we use on Earth for cooking and heating).

Above: Titan is much bigger than our Moon. Unlike our Moon, it has a thick atmosphere.

Methane is just one of several carbon compounds found in the atmosphere. When these carbon compounds break down in the atmosphere, they create an orange smog.

The temperature on Titan is about −180°C. At such a temperature, methane and other carbon gases may turn into liquid and form pools or even oceans on the surface. They may also freeze solid, to form snow and ice.

Looking at Uranus

Uranus is the seventh planet in distance from the Sun, and the third largest. With a diameter of 31,765 miles (51,120 km), it is slightly larger than Neptune. At its closest distance to Earth (about 1.7 billion miles, 2.8 billion km), it can be glimpsed with the naked eye as a very faint star, if you know where in the sky to look for it.

Telescopes show Uranus as a pale greenish-blue disk, with no definite markings. Even close-up pictures of the planet taken by the *Voyager 2* probe in 1986 reveal few features. There are no signs of the bands of clouds seen on Jupiter and Saturn.

Above: William Herschel discovered Uranus in 1781. He also discovered its two largest moons, Titania and Oberon, six years later.

Above: No features can be seen on the face of Uranus. The methane clouds in the atmosphere are hidden by a thick haze.

Right: Makeup of Uranus's atmosphere. Hydrogen, helium, and methane are the main gases.

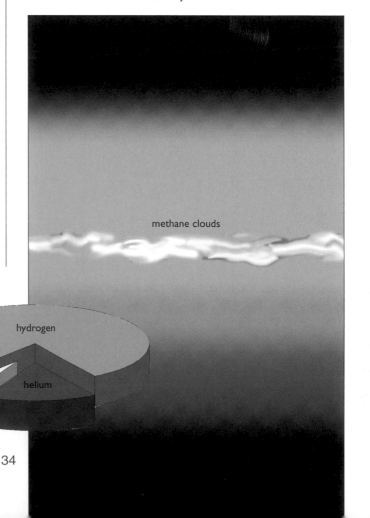

methane clouds

hydrogen

helium

methane

Like most planets, Uranus spins around an axis that is tilted in space as it orbits the Sun. Neptune has a tilted axis, too. Neptune's axis is only slightly tilted, but Uranus's axis tilts so far that the planet travels on its side.

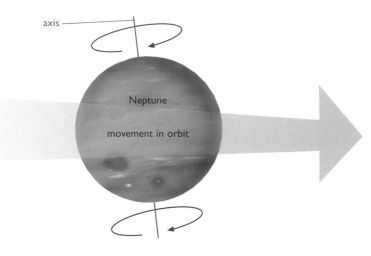

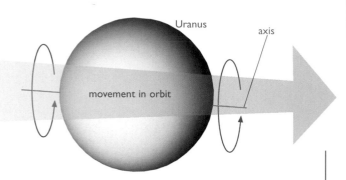

Uranus is a fluid (gas and liquid) planet like Jupiter and Saturn but is different in makeup. It has a very deep atmosphere of hydrogen and helium, with a certain amount of methane. It is the methane that gives the atmosphere its blue-green color.

Beneath the atmosphere, Uranus is covered by a deep, warm ocean that contains water, ammonia, and methane. At its center is a rocky core. Currents swirling in the ocean as the planet spins around create electric currents that make the planet magnetic. Uranus's magnetic force is about as strong as Earth's.

Uranus in Motion

Uranus is so far away that it takes nearly 84 Earth-years to travel once around the Sun. Like the other planets, it spins around in space on its axis, turning around once in about 17 hours.

Most planets rotate in a more or less upright position as they orbit the Sun. But Uranus is different. It spins around on its side. This means that its north and south poles take turns facing the Sun. We do not know why Uranus spins on its side. Maybe

the planet was knocked into this position in a collision with another body long ago.

New Moons

From Earth, we can see five large moons circling around Uranus. William Herschel discovered the first two—Oberon and Titania—in 1797. The others are Miranda, Ariel, and Umbriel.

Voyager 2 took close-up pictures of these moons when it flew past Uranus in 1986. During this mission it also discovered 12 more tiny moons orbiting closer to the planet. The inner two, Cordelia and Ophelia, are the tiniest, measuring only about 15–20 miles (25–30 km) in diameter.

URANUS DATA

Diameter: 31,765 miles (51,120 km)
Average distance from Sun: 1,787,000,000 miles (2,875,000,000 km)
Mass (Earth=1): 15
Density (water=1): 1.3
Spins on axis in: 17.24 days
Circles around Sun in: 83.7 years
Number of moons: 18

Miranda

Umbriel

The five large moons of Uranus, in order of distance from the planet. Their sizes are shown to scale. Smallest is Miranda, which is only about 300 miles (485 km) in diameter.

Titania

Uranus's Large Moons

All of the five large moons of Uranus seem to be made up of a mixture of rock and ice. Titania is the largest, with a diameter of about 980 miles (1,580 km). Its icy surface is pockmarked with craters that measure up to 125 miles (200 km) across. It is crossed by valleys, which are faults, or cracks, in the

surface. One is more than 900 miles (1,500 km) long—more than three times as long as Arizona's famous Grand Canyon.

The slightly smaller Oberon is more heavily cratered, and many of the craters contain dark material. Umbriel is also well cratered and is darker than the other large moons. With a diameter of about 730 miles (1,170 km), it is about the same size as Ariel. Ariel has many craters and networks of deep valleys. It also has large regions of fresh ice, which make it the brightest of the moons.

Miranda, which is about half the size of Ariel, has the most unusual surface of all. It has very different kinds of landscape mixed together, like the different patches in a patchwork quilt. Some regions seem ancient and heavily cratered. Some have strange curving grooves. In other regions ice cliffs soar more than 12 miles (20 km) high.

Rings Around Uranus

Until 1977, Saturn was the only planet known to have rings. In March of that year astronomers accidentally discovered that Uranus also has rings. They were trying to measure the size of the planet accurately by timing how long it took to pass across a distant star. But just before the star passed

Oberon

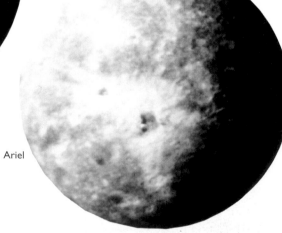

Ariel

behind Uranus, it "winked" several times, showing that something had passed in front of it. The star "winked" again just after it came from behind the planet. Other astronomers carried out similar experiments with the same results—"winks" before and after stars passed behind Uranus. They realized that the "winks" were being caused by sets of rings around the planet.

Voyager 2 pictured the rings clearly in 1986. There are 11 rings in all—10 narrow and relatively bright ones and, inside them, 1 that is very broad but very faint. The rings seem mostly to be made up of lumps of dark material as much as 33 feet (10 meters) in width.

The brightest ring is the outermost one, called the Epsilon. It circles about 15,000 miles (25,000 km) above Uranus's atmosphere. It varies in width between about 12 and 60 miles (20 and 96 km). The other main rings are much narrower, some less than a mile across. The tiny moons Cordelia and Ophelia orbit on either side of the Epsilon ring and seem to act as "shepherds" to keep the ring particles in place.

Above: An artist's impression of Uranus and its rings. In reality, they are dark and difficult to make out.

Below: *Voyager 2* took this close-up picture of Uranus's rings, showing fine dust particles in between the ringlets.

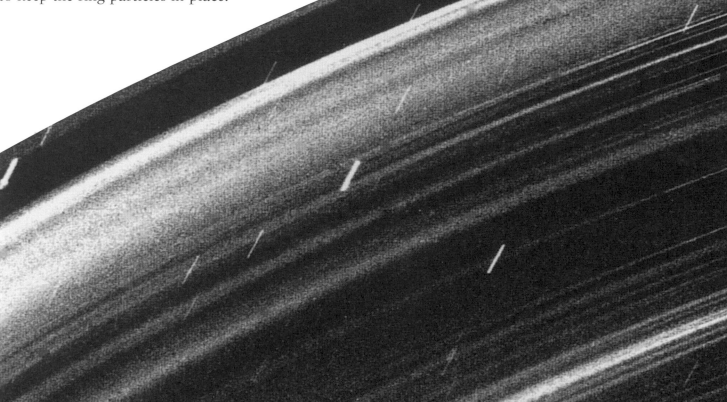

NEPTUNE DATA

Diameter: 30,779 miles (49,530 km)

Average distance from Sun: 2,799,000,000 miles (4,504,000,000 km)

Mass (Earth=1): 17

Density (water=1): 1.6

Spins on axis in: 16.11 days

Circles around Sun in: 163.7 years

Number of moons: 8

Makeup of Neptune's atmosphere. The main gases are hydrogen and helium, with traces of methane.

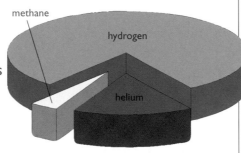

methane

hydrogen

helium

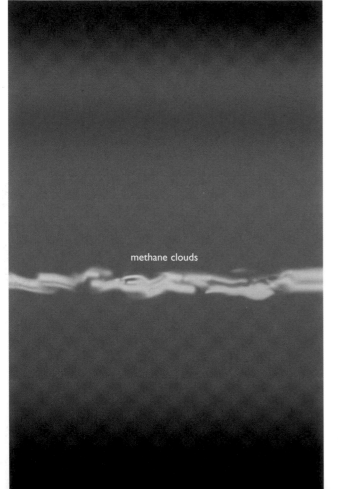

methane clouds

Looking at Neptune

Neptune is a little smaller than Uranus but has much the same makeup, with a thick atmosphere and a warm, deep liquid ocean underneath. It lies about a billion miles (1.6 billion km) farther away from the Sun than Uranus and takes nearly 164 Earth-years to circle the Sun once.

Strangely, even though it is much farther away from the Sun than Uranus, Neptune has more or less the same temperature, about –210°C. This means that Neptune is somehow being heated from within. This internal heat produces much more weather in the atmosphere than we would expect for a planet so far away from the Sun.

Stormy Weather

The main features of Neptune's weather are clouds, winds, and storms. The clouds are white and wispy, like the high cirrus clouds we find on Earth. They are probably made up of crystals of frozen methane.

Winds surge around the planet at high speed, in places reaching 1,500 mph (2,400 km/h) or more. This is five times the speed of winds in the most violent twisters, or tornadoes, on Earth. In places the winds swirl around to form hurricane-like storms. *Voyager 2* spotted several dark oval regions where violent storms were raging. The largest was named the Great Dark Spot. These storm regions had disappeared by the 1990s when the Hubble Space Telescope began photographing the planet.

Neptune's Rings

After finding rings around Uranus, astronomers began to suspect that Neptune

Methane clouds float in Neptune's atmosphere. The upper atmosphere is much less hazy than on Uranus, giving the planet a much deeper blue color.

Like earth, Neptune is a blue planet. On Earth, the color comes from the blue of the oceans. On Neptune, the color comes from the methane in the atmosphere.

Neptune's Moons

The little shepherds are among the six new moons of Neptune found by *Voyager 2*. They seem to be dark, shapeless bodies. Voyager also flew close to Triton, one of the two moons that can be seen from Earth. Triton is a little smaller than our own Moon but is quite a different body. It is a deep-frozen body covered with frozen nitrogen and methane gas. In places icy geysers erupt, shooting fountains of gas and ice high above the surface.

might also have rings around it. This proved to be true. The rings were first pictured clearly by *Voyager 2*, when it visited the planet in 1989.

There are four rings in all—two narrow and bright ones and two that are much broader and fainter. The two bright ones are named Adams and Leverrier after the mathematicians who played key roles in the planet's discovery. The bright Adams is the outermost ring, circling the planet at a distance of about 24,000 miles (40,000 km).

Its ring particles seem to be kept in place by a tiny shepherd moon, named Larissa. Two of the other rings have tiny shepherds, too.

Neptune's rings are named after people who played a part in the planet's discovery. Johann Galle, for example, was the astronomer who first spotted Neptune on September 23, 1846.

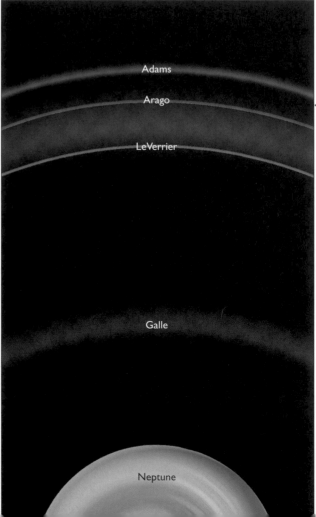

Adams

Arago

LeVerrier

Galle

Neptune

PLUTO AND CHARON

Pluto was the last planet to be discovered. It is the smallest planet by far. Pluto is only about two-thirds the size of our Moon. It is quite different in makeup from all the other planets, consisting mainly of water, ice, and rock. Its only moon, Charon, is half its size.

Neptune was discovered in 1846 after astronomers had found that Uranus was not following the orbit it should. Later, astronomers found that both these planets still orbited in a slightly strange way. So they began to think that there might be yet another planet affecting them.

The first attempts to find a ninth planet were made in the 1870s, but it was not until 1905 that a systematic search began. It was led by the U.S. astronomer Percival Lowell at Flagstaff Observatory in Arizona. Lowell had built the observatory originally to study Mars. The search for the unknown planet, which Lowell called Planet X, revealed nothing by the time of his death in 1916.

It was not until 1929 that the search resumed at Lowell Observatory. A young astronomer from Kansas named Clyde Tombaugh was asked to make and examine photographic plates for new objects in the region where Lowell had thought Planet X might be.

In February 1930, Tombaugh was examining plates he had taken a few weeks earlier and spotted what he was looking for. It was a body far beyond Neptune and much fainter than expected. It was a ninth planet, which came to be called Pluto, after the god of the dark underworld of the dead in Roman mythology.

Astronomers were not able to find out much about Pluto—not even its size—until the 1970s. In 1978, U.S. astronomer James Christy discovered that Pluto had a moon, which was called Charon. By observing the way the moon circled Pluto and using basic laws of motion, astronomers could at last work out Pluto's size and mass. It proved to be just 1,430 miles (2,300 km) in diameter, much smaller than our own Moon. Charon proved to be only half Pluto's size.

The strange thing about the story of Pluto's discovery is that the planet is much too small to have any gravitational effect on Neptune and Uranus. So its discovery seems to have been a lucky accident.

Pluto and its moon, Charon,
pictured at the edge of the solar
system. Here we see them as
crescents, lit up faintly by the
distant Sun, nearly 4 billion miles
(6.4 billion km) away.

The Farthest Planet?

Tiny Pluto is the planet that wanders farthest from the Sun. We cannot say simply that Pluto is the farthest planet, because at times it is not. Between 1979 and 1999, Pluto was actually closer to the Sun than Neptune, and during that time Neptune was the farthest planet.

Pluto wanders inside Neptune's orbit for 20 years of the 248 years it takes to circle once around the Sun. Pluto's orbit is highly elliptical, or oval. As a result, its distance from the Sun varies widely, between about 2.7 and 4.6 billion miles (4.4 and 7.4 billion km).

Pluto's orbit is unusual in another way. Most planets have orbits that lie more or less in the same plane, or flat sheet, in space. But Pluto's orbit reaches high above and below this plane.

Icy World

Pluto is the only planet in the solar system that has not been explored at all by space probes. This means that we know less about it than we do about the other planets.

Pluto is so far away that in telescopes on Earth it looks just like a star, and we can see nothing of its surface. Recently the Hubble Space Telescope has sent back pictures showing some vague light and dark patterns on its surface.

The surface seems to be covered with icy, frozen gases such as nitrogen and methane and even water ice. The light markings we see in the Hubble pictures are probably icy regions. The darker areas might be patches of exposed rock or

Below: Pluto and Charon, photographed from space by the Hubble Space Telescope. No telescopes on the ground are powerful enough to show the two as separate bodies.

Above: We do not know what Pluto really looks like because no space probes have visited it yet. But it could look similar to some of the icy moons of Uranus and Neptune, such as Triton.

Pluto orbit

Neptune orbit

Uranus orbit

Pluto has the most eccentric, or most oval, orbit in the solar system. This orbit takes it way above and below the orbits of the other planets.

they might be regions covered by reddish-brown chemical compounds.

In the feeble heat from the Sun, the surface ice on Pluto slightly evaporates, or turns to gas. This gives the planet a very thin atmosphere. However, this gas turns back to ice as Pluto moves farther from the Sun.

Charon

Pluto's moon, Charon, is so big that Pluto-Charon is often called a double planet. It

Below: Both Pluto and Charon spin around axes that are tilted by the same amount. And both spin round these axes in the same direction, which is the opposite direction to most of the other planets. Pluto and Charon also spin round once in space in the same time—about 6.4 Earth-days.

orbits close to Pluto, at an average distance of less than 12,000 miles (19,000 km). By comparison, our own Moon circles Earth 20 times farther away.

Pluto spins around on its axis once in a little over 6 days. Charon circles around Pluto in exactly the same amount of time. This means that the moon stays fixed in the same position in Pluto's sky.

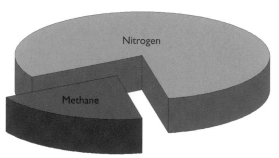

Probable makeup of Pluto's very faint atmosphere.

Nitrogen

Methane

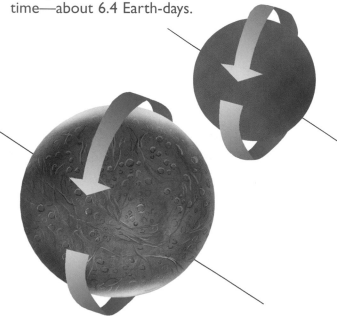

PLUTO DATA

Diameter: 1,429 miles (2,300 km)

Average distance from Sun: 3,676,000,000 miles (5,916,000,000 km)

Mass (Earth=1): 0.002

Density (water=1): 2.0

Spins on axis in: 6.4 days

Circles around Sun in: 248 years

Number of moons: 1

Glossary

ASTEROIDS Small lumps of rock or metal that circle the Sun. Most circle in a broad band (the asteroid belt) between the orbits of Mars and Jupiter.

ATMOSPHERE The layer of gases around Earth or another heavenly body.

AXIS An imaginary line around which a planet or moon spins, or rotates.

BELT A darker band on the face of a gassy planet like Jupiter.

CHASMA A deep valley.

COMET A small icy lump that gives off clouds of gas and dust and starts to shine when it gets near the Sun.

CORE The center part of a body.

CRATER A circular pit in the surface of a planet or moon.

CRUST The hard outer layer of a planet or a moon.

DAY The time it takes a planet to spin around once on its axis in space.

DISK The face of a planet, which we see as a circle in telescopes.

ELLIPTICAL Having the shape of an ellipse; an oval shape.

FALLING STAR A popular name for a meteor.

FAULT A crack in the surface of a planet or moon caused by massive movements in the rocks.

GRAVITY The pull, or force of attraction, that every body has because of its mass.

HEAVENS The night sky; the heavenly bodies are the objects we see in the night sky.

IMPACT CRATER A crater made by the impact (blow) of a meteorite.

INNER PLANETS The four planets relatively close together in the inner part of the solar system—Mercury, Venus, Earth, and Mars.

INTERPLANETARY Between the planets.

INTERSTELLAR Between the stars.

LAVA Molten rock that pours out of volcanoes.

MAGNETIC FIELD The region around a planet or a star in which its magnetism acts.

MANTLE A rocky layer beneath the crust of a rocky planet or moon.

METEOR A streak of light produced when a meteoroid burns up in Earth's atmosphere.

METEORITE A lump of rock from outer space that falls to the ground.

MINOR PLANETS Another name for the asteroids.

MOON The common name for a satellite.

ORBIT The path in space one body follows when it circles around another, such as the Moon's orbit around Earth.

OUTER PLANETS The planets in the outer part of the solar system—Jupiter, Saturn, Uranus, Neptune, and Pluto.

PLANET One of nine bodies that circle around the Sun; or more generally, a body that circles around a star.

PROBE A spacecraft sent to explore other heavenly bodies, such as planets, moons, asteroids, and comets.

RETROGRADE ORBIT An orbit in which a moon travels in the opposite direction of normal.

RINGS Circles of icy or rocky matter around the equators of Jupiter, Saturn, Uranus, and Neptune.

SATELLITE A small body that orbits around a larger one; a moon. Also the usual name for an artificial satellite, an orbiting spacecraft.

SHEPHERD MOON A moon that keeps the particles of a planet's ring in place.

SOLAR Having to do with the Sun.

SOLAR SYSTEM The Sun and the bodies that circle around it, including planets, comets, and asteroids.

STAR A huge ball of very hot gas, which gives off energy as light, heat, and other radiation.

TURBULENCE The churning-up of the gases in an atmosphere.

UNIVERSE Space and everything that is in it—galaxies, stars, planets, moons, and energy.

VOLCANO A hole, or crack in the ground through which molten rock or other material escapes.

YEAR The time it takes a planet to circle once around the Sun.

ZONE A lighter band on the face of a gassy planet like Jupiter.

Important Dates

1610 Galileo discovers the moons of Jupiter and notices something odd about Saturn

1665 Robert Hooke notices the Great Red Spot on Jupiter

1675 Giovanni Cassini discovers a gap in Saturn's ring

1781 William Herschel discovers Uranus

1845 John Couch Adams and Urbain Leverrier separately calculate where another new planet should be found.

1846 Johann Galle discovers Neptune

1894 Percival Lowell builds the Lowell Observatory to study Mars.

1930 Clyde Tombaugh discovers Pluto

1972 First probe to Jupiter launched, *Pioneer 10*

1973 *Pioneer 11* probe launched to Jupiter; *Pioneer 10* reports from Jupiter

1974 *Pioneer 11* reports from Jupiter, sets course for Saturn and is renamed *Pioneer-Saturn*

1977 Astronomers discover Uranus's rings. *Voyager 1* and *2* probes launched to Jupiter and beyond

1978 James Christy discovers Pluto's moon, Charon

1979 *Pioneer-Saturn* flies by Saturn. The Voyager probes report from Jupiter before flying on to Saturn (1980, 1981).

1986 *Voyager 2* makes first visit to Uranus

1989 *Voyager 2* makes first visit to Neptune

1990 Galileo probe launched to Jupiter

1995 Galileo drops probe into Jupiter's atmosphere before going into orbit around the planet.

1997 *Cassini-Huygens* probe launched to Saturn

2004 *Cassini* due to orbit Saturn, *Huygens* to land on Titan

Further Reading

Large numbers of books on astronomy and space are available in school and public libraries. Librarians will be happy to help you find them. In addition, publishers display their books on the Internet, and you can key into their websites and search for astronomy books. Alternatively, you can look at the websites of on-line bookshops (such as Amazon.com) and search for books on astronomy and space. Here are just a selection of recently published books for further reading.

Backyard Astronomy by Robert Burnham, Time-Life, 2001
Comet Science by Jacques Crovisier and Therese Encrenaz, Cambridge, 1999
Exploring the Night Sky with Binoculars by Patrick Moore, Cambridge, 2000
Field Guide to Stars and Planets by Jay Pasachoff, Houghton Mifflin, 1999
Get a Grip on Astronomy by Robin Kerrod, Time-Life, 1999
Introduction to Astronomy by Nick Shaffer, Random House, 1999
Night Sky by Gary Mechler, National Audubon Society, 1999
Observing the Moon by Peter Wlasuk, Springer, 1999
Target Earth by Duncan Steel, Time-Life, 2000
The Young Astronomer by Sheila Snowden, EDC Publications, 2000

Websites

Astronomy and space are popular topics on the Internet, and there are hundreds of interesting websites—details about the latest eclipse, mission to Mars and SETI (Search for Extraterrestrial Intelligence), and so forth.

A good place to start is by using a Search Engine, and search for space and astronomy. Search engines will display extensive listings of topics, which you can then select. For example, you gain access to a list of topics on the Search Engine Yahoo on astronomy with: **http://yahoo.com/Science/Astronomy**

The lists also includes astronomy clubs. If there is one near you, you may wish to join it. Most clubs have interesting programs, with observing evenings, lectures, and visits to observatories.

NASA has many websites covering all aspects of space science, including exploration of the planets and the universe as a whole. The best place to start is at NASA's home page: **http://www.nasa.gov**

From there you can go to, for example, Space Science, which includes planetary exploration. Or you can go directly to: **http://spacescience.nasa.gov/missions**

Individual missions may also have their own website, such as the Mars Odyssey mission at: **http:/mars.jpl.nasa.gov/Odyssey**

The latest information and images from the Hubble Space Telescope can be reached at: **http:/www.stsci.edu/pubinfo** This site will also direct you to picture highlights since the launch of the Telescope in 1990.

European space science activities can be explored via the home page of the European Space Agency at: **http:/www.esa.int**

Index